Don't Bet on It

Adapted by Ann Lloyd

Based on the series created by Michael Poryes and Rich Correll & Barry O'Brien

Part One is based on the episode, "Bad Moose Rising," Written by Steven James Meyer & Douglas Lieblein

Part Two is based on the episode, "My Boyfriend's Jackson and There's Gonna Be Trouble," Written by Andrew Green & Sally Lapiduss

New York

Printed in the United States of America

First Edition
1 3 5 7 9 10 8 6 4 2

Library of Congress Control Number 2007930139
ISBN-13: 978-1-4231-0868-9
ISBN-10: 1-4231-0868-X

For more Disney Press fun, visit www.disneybooks.com
Visit DisneyChannel.com

PART ONE

Chapter One

For once, the house where Miley Stewart lived with her dad, Robby, and her brother, Jackson, was calm and quiet. Her dad was grateful about this, because he was feeling seriously under the weather. Even the birds chirping outside made his head throb.

Unfortunately, the peaceful atmosphere was too good to last. It always is.

The silence was suddenly disrupted by pounding on the front door. Miley's dad, wearing a ratty old robe and blowing his nose, walked slowly down the stairs.

"As if I didn't feel bad enough already," he said with a moan as he saw who his visitor was.

Mr. Dontzig, the Stewarts' next-door neighbor, was standing in the doorway, looking angry. Mr. Stewart reluctantly opened the door and let him in.

"Stewart! I'm sick of your leaves in my pool!" Mr. Dontzig bellowed. He waved a maple leaf in his neighbor's face.

"And I'm sick of your face in my house," Miley's dad said. Then he coughed and turned to collapse onto the couch. Being sick was exhausting.

Mr. Dontzig waved the leaf in the air, trying to fan Mr. Stewart's germs away from him. "Whoa, Jethro!" he said, taking the opportunity to make fun of his neighbor's Southern background. "Since you're not whittling right now, try using your hands to cover your mouth."

Patty, Mr. Dontzig's eight-year-old niece, suddenly poked her head under her uncle's arm. She was wearing a swimsuit, nose clips, goggles, and a floatie.

"Uncle Albert, I wanna swim!" she whined. "What's taking so long? You said the hillbilly was scared of you."

Mr. Dontzig gave Mr. Stewart an icy stare. "He is."

Over on the couch, Miley's dad shivered and pulled his robe tighter around him. He hated being sick, and he was probably the worst patient on the planet.

"See," Mr. Dontzig said to Patty as he imitated Mr. Stewart's shivering. "I've got him trembling."

Patty looked at Mr. Stewart and shrugged. "Come on," she said to her uncle.

"I'm only here for the weekend. You said we'd do stuff."

But Mr. Dontzig couldn't take his eyes off Mr. Stewart. He knew his icy stare was making the guy tremble. "Stop nagging," he said to his niece.

"I wanna do stuff!" Patty cried, stomping her foot.

"Stop nagging!" Mr. Dontzig yelled.

"I wanna do stuff!" Patty whined louder.

"Stop nagging!" Mr. Dontzig said, echoing Patty's whine. He turned to Miley's dad. "I don't know where she gets it from." Then he remembered the reason he'd come over to the Stewarts' in the first place. He threw the large leaf on the ground. "Keep your leaves out of my pool!"

With that, Mr. Dontzig and Patty left.

Miley's dad sighed. Finally, he could get some peace and quiet. He put his achy head down on the couch.

"Dad?" Miley called.

Mr. Stewart looked up to see Miley and Lilly standing over him. "It was nice while it lasted," he mumbled, rubbing his head.

"Dad, why aren't you dressed?" Miley asked. "The Stella Fabiana Fashion Show is tomorrow, and you promised you'd take me and Lilly to the mall to get shoes, makeup, and manicures."

"You did," Lilly added. "I remember. I was there."

Miley and Lilly were very excited about going to the fashion show. Miley had been invited because she was also singing superstar Hannah Montana. Lilly was going with her as Lola, Hannah's best friend. They were sure to see amazing designer clothes and meet other celebrities—but they had to look just right for the event.

Miley tried to get her dad to move. "Come on, come on, let's boogie!"

Mr. Stewart sneezed and grabbed a tissue from his pocket.

"Not that kinda boogie," Lilly said, disgusted.

He blew his nose again, then looked at his daughter. "Sorry, honey, I don't know if I'm going to be able to take you. This thing knocked me flatter than Uncle Earl's inflatable butt cushion after football season."

"Now there's a mental picture I really didn't need," Lilly commented.

"It's okay, Dad," Miley said, giving him a hug. "Feel better. Get well. I'll just make Jackson take us."

After all, thought Miley, what are big brothers for if not to drive their little sisters around town?

But Jackson had heard her from upstairs,

and he had a very different opinion.

"*Noooo!*" Jackson screamed. He slammed his bedroom door and stomped down the stairs. "No, no, no, no, no, no!"

Miley watched her brother as he entered the room and stopped right in front of her.

"Not gonna happen—uh-uh—no way! Cooper and I are going to the Dodger game today. And I'm breakin' in a new foam finger." From behind his back, Jackson pulled out a large, blue foam finger.

"Jackson," Miley said, "Lilly and I have stuff we have to do, and you go to a baseball game practically every week."

"This is so unfair," Jackson whined to his dad. "Every time you can't haul her all over town, I'm the one who gets stuck doing it. I miss baseball games, basketball games, parties. I mean I have a life of my own and . . ." Jackson looked at his little sister. ". . . I'm sick of you ruining it!"

Mr. Stewart's head was throbbing, and his kids' fighting was making him feel worse. He glared at Jackson. "And I'm sick as a dog. Stop complaining. Take your sister where she needs to go. I'll get you tickets to another game."

Jackson sighed. "Fine," he said as he headed for the front door. "Now what am I supposed to do with my new foam finger?" He looked sadly at his blue finger . . . which wouldn't get to go to a game.

"Oh, I know, you can use it to wipe away your tiny little tears," Miley said, wiping a pretend tear from her eye as she and Lilly followed him to the door. She made a boo-hoo face suitable for a three-year-old at Jackson. Then she quickly reverted to her actual age and gave her brother a stern look. "Get over it."

Chapter Two

The next morning, Miley's dad was not feeling any better. Actually, he was feeling worse. He was sitting on the couch wearing his ratty, old robe over pajamas. Next to him was a box of tissues. He sneezed and grabbed a tissue, blowing his nose loud and long. Then he looked into his tissue.

"Oh, why do I always look?" he said with a groan. He crumpled up the tissue and tossed it away.

Miley rushed into the room and sat on the arm of the couch, close but not *too* close to her dad. "Hey, Dad, how are you feeling?"

"Sorry, darling, I don't think I'll be able to take you to that fashion show today," her dad said. He wasn't sure that he could even get off the couch, let alone leave the house.

Miley was sympathetic. Her dad really was looking a little pale. And there was all that snot! "That's okay," she told him. "I'll just make Jackson—"

"NOOOOOOOOOOO!"

Jackson's bedroom door slammed behind him as he came barreling down the hallway and into the living room. "No, no, no, no, no!" he yelled, glaring at his sister. "You already ruined my Saturday. You can't have my Sunday, too."

"Would ya stop whining?" Miley said to

Jackson. "If it wasn't for me, you would've been stuck at that stupid baseball game yesterday. I heard on the news one team didn't even get any hits."

Jackson gritted his teeth, but he couldn't contain himself. "They call it a no-hitter!"

"Exactly," Miley said, quite pleased with herself. *"Bo-ring!"* she sang out.

Jackson wondered how Miley could be so completely clueless about baseball. A no-hitter was unbelievable! He was still trying to recover from the tragedy of not being there—with his new foam finger—to witness the amazing event. He shot Miley a mean look.

Over on the couch, Mr. Stewart coughed a nasty, deep cough.

"Dad, you sound great!" Jackson said, encouraged to see some life in his dad. "You're really gettin' it out!" That gave him a brilliant idea. "And speaking of gettin' out, maybe a little fresh air would do you good! Maybe drive Miley to the fashion show?"

Mr. Stewart got up slowly and began to head back to his bedroom. "No." What he needed right now was his bed and some more rest.

"Come on," Jackson said, "you're just gonna let a little cold beat you?" He egged him on. "You're just gonna abandon your son in his time of need?"

"Yeah," Mr. Stewart muttered as he shuffled his way out of the room.

Jackson couldn't believe that his dad was being so weak. He called after him. "California's made you soft, old man!"

Miley had had enough of Jackson's whining. "I cannot believe how selfish you are," she said, scolding him. "Dad's sick, I need a little help, and all you've done is complain."

"Oh, please," Jackson replied. "If you were me, you'd do exactly the same thing."

"No, you see, Jackson, that's where you're wrong," Miley said. "If I was lucky enough to have a little sister, I'd change my plans when she needed my help. And I'd do it without whining like a little baby."

Jackson didn't believe that for a minute. "Easy to say when you don't actually have a little sister."

"Not my fault," Miley said. "I always wanted one." She turned and walked out of the room.

"And I wanted a puppy," Jackson called out, "but they brought you home instead!"

"Too bad!" Miley shouted as she went to her bedroom.

Just then, there was a knock at the front

door. Mr. Dontzig appeared in the door-way, sneezing and waving a tissue. Next to him was his niece, Patty.

"Your father gave me his backwoods cold," Mr. Dontzig said to Jackson accusingly. "Yesterday, I was the picture of health. Now look at me. I'm withering away to nothing." He opened his robe and extended his arms, revealing his rather large gut hanging over his pajama pants.

Jackson looked at Mr. Dontzig's pro-truding belly. "On the bright side," he said, "maybe you'll see your toes by Christmas."

Annoyed, Mr. Dontzig wrapped his robe tightly around his middle. "Listen, Junior," he grumbled. "I'm stuck with my niece for the weekend, and now I'm too sick to schlep her around." He pushed Patty into the house. "So congratulations, you've won an eight-year-old for the day."

"Whoa," Jackson said, stepping back. "I don't think so."

Patty walked up to Jackson and looked him straight in the eye. "Are you going to grow anymore, or is that it?" she asked.

Jackson didn't like people making fun of his height or, rather, his lack of it. He frowned and pushed Patty toward the door. "Okay, buh-bye."

"Stewart, please, please, I'm begging here," Mr. Dontzig pleaded. "What do you want me to do, get down on my knees?"

"Look, there's no way I'd put up with this brat for a whole day," Jackson said, eyeing Patty. He gestured behind him. "I've already got one upstairs who . . ." And then Jackson got his second brilliant idea of the day. ". . . always wanted a little sister," he finished. He tapped Patty on the head. "And you are perfect." Smiling, he called out, "Hey, Mile! I've got a present for you!"

"I don't know what you're up to," Mr. Dontzig said. "And I don't care. Have her home by dinner. If I'm not there, stick her in the mail slot!" Mr. Dontzig left quickly before Jackson's plans changed.

Digging into his pocket, Jackson held out a five dollar bill to Patty. "Here's five bucks," he said. "Just keep your mouth shut for two minutes."

"Make it ten and you've got a deal, leprechaun," Patty responded.

The kid was smart. And Jackson was desperate. So he took out another five dollar bill and gave it to Patty. If his plan went as he thought, the money would be well spent.

Miley ran down the steps into the living room. "What present? What are you talking about?" she asked. Then she noticed Patty. "Hey, who's this?" She gave Patty a big smile. "Hey, sweetie, what's your name?"

True to her word, and her bribe, Patty didn't say a thing.

Jackson stepped forward, putting his arm around the girl. "Patty. She's Dontzig's niece and your new little sister for the day."

Miley's smile disappeared from her face. "What?"

"He's sick, she needs a babysitter, and you said you always wanted a little sister. Ta-da!" Jackson was enjoying the look of surprise on his sister's face. Yup, ten dollars well spent.

"You've got two wishes left. If you need me, I'll be in the lamp," he said as he headed for the refrigerator to get a soda.

Patty wished that her two minutes of

silence were over, but a deal was a deal and money was money. She covered her mouth with both hands to keep her end of the bargain.

Watching Patty, Miley sensed something was up. She looked over at Jackson. "What's wrong with her?"

As Jackson opened a can of soda, he called back to Miley. "She's shy."

Miley grew very sympathetic. "Oh, that's so cute." She leaned in closer to Patty. "Sorry, sweetheart, I already made plans." She pointed to Jackson and added, "Which someone knew about."

"Oh, you've got plans," Jackson said. He moved closer to Miley. "Kinda like I had to give up yesterday for you?"

Miley got in Jackson's face. "That's not fair, the fashion show is a once-in-a-lifetime thing."

"So was the no-hitter!" Jackson yelled, staring his sister down. "The truth is, you're just too selfish to give up one day of your life for this sweet, innocent little girl, the way I always do for you."

"That's so not true," Miley declared.

"Oh, please, you wouldn't last one day with this kid," Jackson said, challenging his sister.

"Oh, yeah?" Miley countered.

"Doing whatever she wants without a single complaint," Jackson said, making sure Miley knew the rules.

"You wanna bet?" Miley asked.

"Yeah, I do," Jackson said. "Right now." He walked over to stand behind Patty.

"But you know I've got to go to that fashion show," Miley said.

Jackson knew that Miley was struggling with the decision. She never backed down from a dare, but she also was really looking forward to the fashion show. Which way would she go? Jackson saw Patty looking at her watch. The kid was going to pipe up any second, and who knew what she might say? He had to act fast.

He leaned closer to Miley. "Coward. Gutless. Chicken." Then, for good measure, he added, "Cowardly, gutless chicken."

That did it! *No one* got away with calling her a cowardly, gutless chicken!

"Okay, okay, fine! I'll give up my fashion show," she shouted. "But when I win, which I will, you have to drive me around wherever I want to go, whenever I want to go, without complaint, for the rest of my nondriving life!"

"And when you don't, which you won't, I'm free. Forever," Jackson said, already tasting the sweetness of victory. "Whatever she wants. No complaints," he added, just to be clear.

"Deal," Miley said.

"Deal," Jackson agreed. He looked at his watch and counted down the seconds. "Three . . . two . . . one."

Suddenly, Patty had a chance to use her voice again. "Make me a sandwich, or I'll scream," she demanded.

Miley looked at Patty with wide eyes. "What?"

"*Aaaaaaaahh!*" Patty opened her mouth wide and let out a loud scream.

Miley knew she had been had. "You set me up," she said to Jackson.

A smile spread across Jackson's face. "Do I hear a complaint?" he said, cupping his hand behind his ear. "Do we already have a winner?"

"Forget it. I'm not caving," she said. "I'm

going to get through this afternoon, and for dinner I'm going to serve a big slice of humble pie."

Patty stood with her arms tightly folded across her chest. "You know what I want to watch?" she yelled. "You making me my sandwich! Now close your mouth and open the fridge, I'm not getting any younger!"

Miley looked down at the pigtailed little girl. "Okay, listen here, kid, I've only got one thing to tell you. . . ." Before Miley finished her sentence she caught her brother's eye. She did not want to lose this bet within the first five minutes! She turned back to Patty and flashed her a huge smile. "White or wheat?"

Chapter Three

Later that day, when Jackson and Miley were both out of the house, Mr. Stewart finally got to enjoy some peace and quiet. He was lying on the couch in the living room when his moment of relaxation was disrupted by a phone call. He kept his arm draped over his eyes as he spoke into the phone.

"Roxy, you don't need to come over," he said. "I'm feeling much, much better."

At that moment, Roxy walked into the

living room talking on her cell phone and carrying an overnight bag. She saw Mr. Stewart lying on the couch and stood right behind him. "Is that so?" she asked.

With his eyes covered, Miley's dad didn't see Roxy standing in his house. He continued to weave his web of lies, trying to get her to believe he wasn't sick. "Yes, ma'am. As a matter of fact, I was just heading out for a jog now."

"Then why are you lying on the couch in that ratty old robe?" Roxy asked.

"How did you . . ." he began. Then he moved his arm and looked up to see Hannah Montana's bodyguard hovering above him.

"You can't lie to Roxy," she said. "Roxy knows everything. I'm omniscient, omnipresent and omnipotent—look 'em up, country boy."

Mr. Stewart knew that Roxy's heart was in the right place, but she wasn't hired to be his nurse. "Roxy, I appreciate it," he said, "but your job isn't to take care of me, it's to be Hannah Montana's bodyguard."

She shrugged as she batted that idea away with her hand. "That's just the fever talking. You know we're just like family." She started to organize her things. "Now, just let Aunt Roxy take care of those nasty, nasty germs."

"But what if you get sick?" he asked.

"Ha! Roxy ain't afraid of no germs, germs are afraid of Roxy," she said. "Now, the first thing we're gonna do is get you in the shower, steam those suckers out, and open up those pores!" She pulled up Mr. Stewart and got a whiff of him. "Plus, you are a little ripe."

Mr. Stewart made a face. "That's the

smell of fear," he confessed. "Besides," he added, looking at the steps toward his bedroom, "I can't make it up the stairs."

"That's where sixty hours of firefighter training comes in handy," Roxy told him. "Now just relax and enjoy the ride." With that, Roxy threw him over her shoulder and headed upstairs as if he were being rescued from a burning building.

"Put me down! Stop it!" Mr. Stewart yelled, but it was no use. Once Roxy had a plan, it was hard to distract her. "Why did I give you a house key-ey-ey-ey-ey?" he cried as Roxy jogged up the stairs.

At Rico's beachside snack bar, Jackson was enjoying eating a hot dog—and watching the scene in front of him. So far, Miley had done everything that Patty had asked. He knew that his little sister was probably close to her breaking point . . . and he couldn't wait for that moment!

Jackson leaned close to his sister. "How's it going so far, Mile?" Miley's head was the only part of her not covered in sand. Patty had buried her on the beach.

Jackson was gleeful. He was definitely going to win this bet! "Any complaints?" he asked.

Miley gave her brother a forced smile as Patty happily shoveled more sand on top of her. "No," Miley said. "After she ran over me with her Boogie board and threw up on me in the kayak, ya know, this is actually kind of relaxing." Then she felt a little bite on her leg. "Except for the sand crabs," she added. "But I'm not complaining."

"Glad to hear it," Jackson said, although he didn't really believe her. He looked over at Patty. "Hey, Patty, want some ice cream?"

She jumped up and down. "Yeah," she said. She took Jackson's hand, eager to go off in search of a nice cold treat.

"Wait!" Miley called. She slowly started to get up. Being buried in the sand was getting old, not to mention itchy. "Patty, can I get up now?"

Jackson leaned down and whispered in Patty's ear. She smiled and faced Miley.

"No way," she said. "When I get back, I want to take a picture." Then she barked another order. "And don't move!"

Miley resumed her buried position, covering herself back up with sand.

"You heard her," Jackson said. "Don't move!"

"And just remember, I'm still going to win the bet," Miley whispered to Jackson.

Jackson smirked. "As long as you don't move." Before he left with Patty, he couldn't resist giving his buried sister some advice. "Try not to think about the sand crabs."

"Not thinking," Miley said, trying not to dwell on her itchy arms and legs. "I'm not thinking," she said again with conviction. Then she felt something. "Ow, that was a big one!"

When Patty and Jackson finally came back from eating ice cream, Miley did everything the little girl wanted. First, she wanted Miley to pull her around on in-line skates. So Miley attached a rope around her waist and Patty held on to the other end. Miley pulled her along the boardwalk like a horse pulling a carriage.

Soon Patty noticed a group of people flying kites. Miley got a kite for Patty and tried to get it up in the air. She went running across the basketball courts, trying desperately to catch the wind. Because Miley was keeping her eye on the kite, looking for some sign of movement, she wasn't watching where she was going—and she ran right off the dock into the water!

Jackson couldn't help but laugh. This was totally ten dollars well spent! Seeing his sister get all wet made him think of another idea. He whispered into Patty's ear, and soon Miley's face was sticking out of a mermaid cutout—a perfect target for water balloons! Patty took a couple of shots, and then she allowed Jackson to try. With perfect aim, he nailed his target. Still trying to be a good sport, Miley gave them both a huge, soaking-wet smile.

Just a few more hours, Miley thought. It will all be worth it when I win this bet! Then I can get back to my life!

Chapter Four

While Miley was in a sweat trying to win the bet by doing everything Patty demanded, her dad was literally sweating. Roxy had gotten him into a reflective sweatsuit that made him look like he was wrapped in tinfoil. He was lying under the hot sun on a lounge chair in the yard.

"Roxy," he said, "how long do I have to stay in this thing?" He had felt so lousy earlier that he was willing to try her crazy idea. But this was insanity! He was melting!

Taking a sip of her fruity tropical drink, Roxy leaned over from her seat next to Mr. Stewart. She pulled out a meat thermometer from under his armpit. "Oh, honey, you're just medium rare. We're looking to get you all the way to well done!" She glanced at her watch. "Look at that, I've been so busy taking care of you, I almost forgot about lunch."

She grabbed a can of cooking spray from the table next to her and sprayed it on Mr. Stewart's tinfoil-covered chest.

"What're you doin'?" he cried.

Roxy paid no attention to him. She placed a hamburger patty on his chest. "I hate it when my meat sticks to my pan, or in this case, my *man*."

The patty started to sizzle, and Miley's

dad sighed. The road to good health was painful!

Later that day at Rico's, Oliver sat next to Miley. They were watching Patty, who was sitting at the snack counter with Jackson. The little girl looked very tired, which Miley thought was a good sign. She was sure the day was finally nearing an end.

Oliver shoved a spoonful of ice cream in his mouth, swallowed, and turned to Miley. "I don't understand why you don't just dump the kid and go home?"

Watching her friend inhale his bowl of ice cream, she said, "And I don't understand why you eat with your face." Then she got down to the issue at hand. "I'm not dumping her because I'm winning the bet!" She pointed to a sleepy Patty, drooped over the counter. "Look at her."

Patty shifted in her chair and looked at Jackson. "I'm tired," she whined. "I want to go back to Uncle Albert's."

Oliver stuck a straw in his bowl of ice cream and slurped up the last remains of his snack. Miley hit him on the arm to focus his attention.

"Watch this. I'm gonna win the bet and go to my fashion show," Miley said. "Any minute she's gonna come over here and say . . ."

Just at that moment, Patty walked over to Miley. "I want to go home," she said.

Miley jumped up and down. She had won! "Yes!" she shouted.

"No!" Jackson cried.

"Game *ovah*!" Miley declared. She pulled Jackson aside. "I was this close to cracking, but I didn't." Then she did a little victory dance with a song. *"She's done, I* won . . ." Miley sang. *"I didn't cave, now you're my slave. And I can go to the fashion show. Hahahaha!"*

Miley took Patty's hand and led her toward the parking lot. But Jackson grabbed Patty's other hand.

"Whoa, slow down, Busta Rhymes," Jackson said to his sister. Then he turned to Patty. "You can't go home yet. There's got to be something more you want to do."

Just then, a little boy and his mother walked by them. The boy was carrying a stuffed moose. This gave Jackson his third brilliant idea of the day!

"What about a moose?" he asked. "From the world-famous Make-a-Moose store!"

Patty's eyes lit up. Suddenly, she seemed to have more energy. "They've got a Make-a-Moose here?!"

Jackson nodded. He knew that he had

set an irresistible trap. All kids loved the stores where you could create your own stuffed moose.

"Are you kidding?" Oliver chimed in. "It's one of the biggest in the country. My brother goes there all the time. He loves it!"

Miley glared at her friend. How could he be helping Jackson? "Oliver. She doesn't want to go there." Looking at Patty, Miley said, "Honey, you don't want to go there. It's just a bunch of hot, sweaty, screaming kids fighting over moose parts."

"Doesn't that sound like fun?" Jackson asked. "And don't forget that cute little song." The Make-a-Moose theme song was sung to the tune of "Row, Row, Row Your Boat." Jackson belted out the lyrics enthusiastically.

Oliver couldn't help himself. He started to sing along with Jackson.

"Oliver!" Miley scolded.

He shrugged. "I'm sorry. It's catchy."

Miley leaned toward Patty. "Honey, didn't you say you were tired? Wouldn't you rather just go home and relax and just watch some TV?"

That did sound like a good idea to Patty. After all, she had been out doing stuff all day. And she *was* tired. "Well . . ." she said.

Jackson quickly stepped in.

"Or, you could go home later and watch TV, cuddled up with your new best friend . . . Moosey . . ." He paused as he tried to think of a cute name for a moose. Under pressure, he blurted out, ". . . McMooserpants." He gave Patty a shoulder hug. "That's what you really want to do."

"No," Miley said, taking Patty's arm. "What you really want to do is go home and relax. Ahhh."

Jackson took Patty's other arm. "Make-a-Moose. Oooh!" he cooed.

"Home and relax. Ahhh!" Miley said, pulling Patty toward her.

"Make-a-Moose. Oooh!" Jackson said.

Patty looked from Miley to Jackson. "I think I want to go . . ."

Miley and Jackson held their breath as they waited for Patty's decision.

"Make-a-Moose!" she shouted excitedly.

Miley looked like a deflated balloon. "Ahhh!" she said.

She had been so close to winning! But she wasn't going to give up now. One quick moose, and Miley would be on her way to winning the bet—and to making the fashion show!

Chapter Five

The Make-a-Moose store was a complete zoo! Tons of people were crammed inside, all searching for the perfect items to create the perfect moose. As Miley, Jackson, and Patty entered the store, two kids were wrestling over a moose. Miley had a headache already, and they hadn't been in the store for more than a minute. She also quickly understood why Oliver had broken into the Make-a-Moose song. Not only was it catchy, it was the only music the store played!

Patty didn't seem to notice any of this, though. She looked delighted. "This is so cool!" she cried as she ran off to explore all her moose-making options.

"And it's even noisier than I thought," Jackson said. He looked over at Miley. She was rubbing her head. Jackson smiled. "What's the matter, you got a headache?"

"No, I'm just seeing where my antlers would go if I had them," Miley replied.

All of a sudden, Patty and another kid got in a fight over a moose. Miley sighed. This was going to take way too long, unless she managed to speed up the process. She ran to the bin with the unstuffed moose and pulled one out. She was determined to get Patty to make her moose in record time and then to get her out the door.

Just then, a moose call sounded throughout the store, and everyone turned to see Moosemaster Mike, a slow-talking, slow-moving guy in a moose suit, complete with soft antlers. He spoke into a megaphone, greeting all the customers. "All first-time moose makers, meet in the clearing," he said, gesturing to a corner of the store.

"Come on, let's go!" Patty exclaimed, dragging Miley with her.

Moosemaster Mike led the group of kids and parents in the Make-a-Moose theme song. In the midst of all the noise, Miley barely heard her cell phone ring. Just in time, she looked down and saw the call was from Lilly!

Miley felt a little jealous as she thought of Lilly, dressed as Hannah Montana's friend Lola, sitting at the fashion show and seeing all the great new clothes. She flipped open her phone. "Lilly, I don't want to hear how incredible the fashion show is."

Lilly had to strain to hear Miley over the loud techno music at the show. She was sitting in the front row, watching a parade of models march by and loving every minute of it.

"Okay," Lilly said. "Then I won't tell you how celebrity model Lindsay Lohan twisted her ankle. Isn't that great?"

"Why is that great?" Miley asked. Twisting an ankle is a huge bummer, she thought.

"Because," Lilly explained, "they told me if Hannah Montana could get here before the finale, she could fill in and keep the one of a kind . . ." Lilly couldn't help herself. She started to squeal in delight. She finally squeaked out, ". . . Stella Fabiana dress!"

Miley looked over at Patty, who was totally engrossed in what Moosemaster Mike had to say. Leaving early didn't look like an option anymore. "Lilly, I don't want to hear about this."

But Lilly had an ace up her sleeve—or rather in her cell phone. "I'm sending you a picture now."

"And I don't want to see it, either," Miley protested. But when the photo of the dress flashed on her cell-phone screen, she couldn't help it—she just had to take a look. "Aww, it is beautiful! Why are you doing this to me?"

Jackson appeared at Miley's shoulder. He looked at the photo on her phone screen. "Oooh, pretty," he said. "If I were you, I would do anything to own that dress. That precious, precious dress."

Miley didn't want to admit it, but she

was cracking. She had done everything that Patty wanted all day long—but now she had the chance to be in a fashion show wearing an awesome, one-of-a-kind dress! How could she turn that down?

Jackson could sense that Miley was waffling. To the tune of the all-too-familiar Make-a-Moose song, he sang, *"Give, give, give up the bet, give it up right now. . . ."*

Hearing Jackson sing that taunting ditty snapped Miley back into competitive mode. "No, no, no. I'm going to win the bet and get that dress." She spoke into the phone. "Lilly, tell Stella I'll be there faster than you can say Make-a-Moose."

Of course, Lilly didn't know that Miley was stuck at the moose-making store, so she was totally confused by this comment. "Why would Stella Fabiana say 'Make-a-Moose'?"

"Just tell her I'll be there!" Miley cried and hung up the phone. She went over to Patty. "Okay, Patty, let's goose this moose!"

Before Miley could take Patty to a moose station, Moosemaster Mike walked over to them. Jackson seized the moment. He could see that Miley was plotting how to get out of the store quickly, so he asked Moosemaster Mike a question—a question he knew would take him a long time to answer. "You said there were over a hundred different moose types," Jackson said innocently. "Could you name them all?"

A self-assured grin spread across Moosemaster Mike's face. "Of course," he answered.

Miley gave Jackson an angry look. "You better learn to sleep with your eyes open," she hissed.

Moosemaster Mike held up a stuffed

moose sporting a karate outfit. "Number one. Moose Lee. 'Hi-ya'," he said, moving one little arm in a karate chop.

As he went on—and on and *on*—Miley tried not to think about the gorgeous dress waiting for her at the show. When she looked up again, Moosemaster Mike was showing everyone a stuffed moose holding a light sword. "Number twenty-three. Moose Skywalker. 'May the forest be with you'," he said.

Man, thought Miley, at this rate I'll never get to walk the runway. She was quickly running out of time—and patience.

Miley didn't know it, but her dad was running out of patience as well. He was tired of feeling sick, tired of blowing his nose, and tired of suffering through Roxy's crazy schemes to get him well. As he sat at the kitchen table wearing his pajamas and robe, Roxy stirred a pot on the stove. Like a gourmet chef, she put a drop from the spoon on her wrist to test the temperature. Then she leaned over and took a big sniff.

"Bam!" she exclaimed. "Mmm-mmm, perfect." She took the pot over to the table. "Roxy's not-too-hot pot of burnin' funk," she declared. "Oh, yeah. You don't want your funk too hot or too cold, you want your funk just right." Then she looked at her patient. "Now get ready."

Miley's dad already felt a little queasy, so he definitely was not interested in eating what Roxy had cooked up. But he tried to be polite. "It looks delicious, Roxy," he said, "but I'm just not hungry."

"Oh, honey," Roxy said. "You don't eat the funk, the funk eats you." She pulled a sponge out of the pot, and slopped the greenish goo on Mr. Stewart's chest.

"Whoa!" he screamed. "What are you doing?" He looked at the gross goo on his chest. Then he inhaled. "Hey, my sinuses, they're opening up. I can finally breathe." He looked at Roxy. "What's that horrible smell?"

Roxy smiled widely. "That's the funk!"

Chapter Six

At Make-a-Moose, Moosemaster Mike was still listing the many celebrity moose stuffed animals. When Miley tuned back in, Mike was holding up a stuffed moose with a red wig.

"Number forty-nine. I Love Moosey," he said. Using his best Spanish accent, he tried to sound like Ricky Ricardo from the old television show, *I Love Lucy*. He looked right at the redheaded moose and said, "'Oh, Moosey, I'm home!'"

Everyone sitting around Moosemaster Mike laughed. Everyone except Miley. This was no longer a laughing matter. Time was ticking away—and so was her chance to wear that Stella Fabiana dress.

Jackson saw his opening. Miley was definitely at the end of her rope. "Fifty more?" he asked. If Moosemaster Mike listed fifty more moose identities, Miley would certainly miss her show. "Or you could quit now and get to Stella."

"Forget it. I'm not quittin'!" Miley barked. She took Patty's hand. "Come on, Patty, we're making a moose!"

Miley knew the drill. She had made a moose before. She grabbed a moose and went over to the stuffing machine.

Moosemaster Mike stopped his recitation as he watched Miley walk off. "Please stay with the herd," he said.

"Tell it to someone who cares, Bullwinkle," she said.

With lightning speed, Miley took charge of Patty's moose-making project. She was a blur as she raced to each of the stations, madly creating a moose. In record time, Miley produced a moose and handed it to Patty. It was a moose with a blonde wig and a microphone. "Here ya go," she said. "Hannah Moosetana!"

Jackson peered over at the moose. "How lame."

But Patty was delighted. "She's perfect!" she squealed.

"Ha!" Miley laughed.

"Except she needs more stuffing," Patty said, pouting.

"Ha!" Jackson said.

Now Miley was really annoyed. She gave her brother a mean look. "I'd like to stuff something all right."

Jackson smiled sweetly. "Complaining?"

"No!" Miley told him. "Of course not."

Miley took Hannah Moosetana to the stuffing machine and hooked the stuffing tube up to the back of the moose. She flipped the machine on. The stuffing was moving too slowly, so she banged the machine. "Come on, faster, faster!"

Miley poured more and more stuffing into the moose.

"Turn it off!" Patty cried in dismay. "My moose is getting too big!"

Miley tried to stop the stuffing machine, but she couldn't! "Ah, man," she said. "It won't shut off!"

Patty pulled her Hannah Moosetana off the tube and stuffing went flying everywhere. People started to point and stare.

"Abusing the stuffer will result in confiscation of your moose," Moosemaster Mike warned.

Miley, hoping to hide the spewing tube, shoved it into the back of her pants and struck a casual pose. "There was no moose abuse. We were just looking," she said. Then she addressed the growing crowd around her. "Go about your business, please."

She tried to sound calm, but she could feel her pants filling up with stuffing. If she didn't turn off the machine soon, she was going to be a stuffed moose herself!

Jackson noticed Miley's problem with delight. "Wait, I have a question . . ." he said to Moosemaster Mike.

"No, you don't," Miley said.

"Yes, I do," Jackson calmly replied. "I was just wondering, what is the difference between a moose and a caribou?"

Moosemaster Mike became very excited. "That's my favorite question!" he cried. "First of all, the moose is larger. Much, much larger."

"Well, then maybe my moose should be bigger!" Patty demanded.

"Your moose is fine," Miley said, still struggling with the hose in her pants.

"But he said . . ." Patty started to whine.

Miley cut her off. "I don't care what he said! I've done enough for you!" she screamed. "I'm sick of this! I have my own life! And I'm not going to let you ruin it!"

"That's it! I win!" Jackson said with glee. "You blew up!"

"I did not blow up!" Miley cried. But just as the words left her mouth, the amount of stuffing in her pants hit the limit—and they exploded! "Now I blew up," she said sadly.

"You know," Jackson said. "When I pictured winning the bet, I never quite pictured it like this."

"Really? That's funny," Miley said. "I always pictured myself with my pants blowing off and being forced to wear an itchy moose suit."

After Miley's stuffing explosion, Moosemaster Mike gave her a moose costume to wear since her pants were in shreds. Jackson and Miley were sitting on the floor of the store while Patty played happily with her Hannah Moosetana.

Moosemaster Mike walked by and saw Miley sitting with Jackson. "Remember, it's a loaner," he said, referring to his prized moose costume.

Miley looked over at Jackson. "Is lugging me around really as awful as what you put me through today?"

"Yes," he said. Then he saw the sad look in Miley's eyes. It seemed as if she really had learned her lesson. He sighed. "No, but sometimes it feels that way. You know the part that bothers me the most?"

"No," Miley said.

"You never even ask," Jackson told her. "You just kind of expect it. And you never say thanks."

Miley had to agree with him. "You're right. I don't."

"But since I won the bet," Jackson said, "I guess we don't have to worry about it anymore."

"Yeah, I guess not," Miley said. He had won the bet fair and square. "And Jackson, I'm really sorry for all the things you had to miss because of me."

Jackson stood up. "Thanks. Now, we better get a move on if we're going to drop off Patty, get to that fashion show, and get you that dress."

Miley stood up quickly. "What?"

"Well, it's different when I offer," he said. "Then I'm doing it because I want to, not because I have to."

Miley gave her big brother a giant moose hug.

"Miles," Jackson said, "you don't have to do that."

"I know," she said with a smile. "I'm doing it because I want to. And thanks."

They hugged again.

"You're welcome," Jackson told her. He looked over at Patty. "Come on, Patty, let's go."

As they all headed for the door, Patty

turned to Miley and Jackson. "This was the best day ever! I'm so glad Uncle Albert pretended to be sick!"

"What?!" Jackson and Miley said at the same time.

"Oops," Patty said, putting her hand over her mouth.

Chapter Seven

The room was packed with reporters and celebrities. They were all excitedly waiting to see the final spectacular dress in Stella Fabiana's newest collection. Lilly, dressed as Lola, was sitting in the front row. Jackson slid into a seat next to her.

"I can't believe you guys made it!" Lilly cried. "She's gonna look so good in that dress! Then she gets to keep it."

Jackson shrugged. "If she can get in it," he said.

Lilly turned to Jackson, concerned. "Why would she not be able to get in it?"

"When I left her backstage," he whispered, "she was having a little problem with the stuck zipper."

Lilly had seen the dress. She was confused. "There's no zipper on that dress."

"I'm not talking about the dress," Jackson said.

The lights dimmed and an announcement boomed through the speakers. "And now, adding her own unique style to a Stella Fabiana original . . . celebrity model Hannah Montana!"

When Lilly saw her best friend, she was shocked. "What the heck is that?" she cried as Miley strutted down the runway.

"It's what all the moose are wearing in

Part One

"It's okay, Dad," Miley said. "Feel better. Get well.
I'll just make Jackson take us."

"Deal," Miley and Jackson said together.

"And just remember, I'm still going to win the bet,"
Miley whispered to Jackson.

Oliver couldn't help himself. He started to sing the
Make-A-Moose theme song along with Jackson.

"If I were you," said Jackson, "I would do anything to own that dress."

"There was no moose abuse," Miley said. "We were just looking. Go about your business, please."

"You know," Jackson said, "when I pictured winning the bet, I never pictured it quite like this."

"Adding her own unique style to a **Stella Fabiana** original . . . celebrity model Hannah Montana!" the announcer said.

Oh, no! Paulie the photographer sold his photo to a tabloid newspaper.

"I am not going to some stupid celebrity party as Hannah's little show dog," Jackson said.

"Where's the press?" Miley asked as she looked around the party.

"I love you, Hannah Montana, and I never want to break up with you—ever, ever!" Jackson cried.

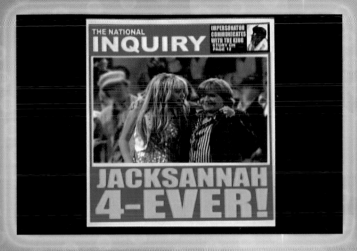

The next morning, a choice photo of the new hot couple graced the papers again.

With each event, Jackson got more into his role as Hannah's boyfriend.

"If I'm not seen in public wearing the sunglasses, the jacket, and the watch," Jackson argued, "I'm going to have to give them all back."

On the set of the *Wake Up, It's Wendy!* show, Hannah Montana was singing, "If We Were a Movie."

Paris this year," Jackson said, laughing.

Miley walked as gracefully as she could. The dress was shiny, gold, and fabulous . . . even though it was stretched over a moose suit!

The next day, Jackson was lying on the couch, watching television. He looked up to see his dad come down the stairs, dressed in a jogging suit and closely followed by Roxy.

"Thanks, Roxy," Mr. Stewart said. "I haven't felt this good in years."

"Any time, sugar," Roxy replied. "Seeing that bounce in your step is all the reward I need."

"Well, I'm just gonna go out for a run, so . . . please, don't feel like you have to wait here for me," Mr. Stewart said. "Please. Don't."

"Let me just collect my lotions and

potions," Roxy said. "And sorry about that pot. I guess even cast iron can't stand up to Roxy's funk."

She went into the kitchen to get all her things. When she was out of the room, Mr. Stewart leaned on the couch for support. He really wasn't feeling any better, but he had to send Roxy home. Her get-healthy regimen was killing him!

"You sure you're okay, Dad?" Jackson asked.

"I feel horrible, son," he whispered. "But if I don't get that woman outta here, she's gonna nurse me to death."

As the words left his mouth, Mr. Stewart sensed that he was doomed. Roxy was standing right behind him holding her infamous tinfoil sweatsuit.

"What part of 'Roxy hears everything' don't you understand?" she demanded.

"Now put on your suit, Tin Man. I'm throwin' my hot stones on the grill and a porterhouse on your chest!"

"Oh, can we have some of your great homemade soup with that? Roxy soup?" Jackson asked.

"What soup?" Roxy said. Then she realized with horror what Jackson had done. "Ah, no, the boy ate the funk. Hold on, Jackson, I'm gonna brew up a pot of antifunk."

"Antifunk?" Jackson asked. What were they talking about? Though he did kind of feel a bit funky after that soup snack .

PART TWO

Chapter One

The Hannah Montana concert was hopping. Hannah was center stage, doing her second encore. It was one of her favorite numbers, "I Got Nerve." At the end of the song, she waved to the screaming crowd, yelled out her thanks, and ran off-stage.

At the stage door, a limo was waiting to take the superstar home. Also waiting were lots of loving fans!

Jackson, wearing his baseball cap and sunglasses, helped Miley, still dressed as Hannah Montana, get through the crowd and into the limo.

"Thanks for coming! See you next time!" Miley called to her fans. "I love you all!"

Jackson kept getting pushed as he steered his sister to the car. "Take it easy, people," he said. "She picks her nose like everybody else. One nostril at a time." He shut the door on the enthusiastic crowd.

Miley rolled down the window. "That's not true!" she yelled.

"Right," Jackson said. "She has people do it for her!" he shouted. Then he reached across his sister and rolled up the window as the car began to move.

"Hey, it was one time!" Miley insisted. She remembered the one instance very well. "My nails were wet, and Lilly offered."

She leaned forward to speak to Andy, her limo driver. "Andy, don't bother with switching limos. Nobody's following us, and the sooner I stop breathing the same air as my brother, the better."

"Lighten up, I'm just having a little fun," Jackson said. He was feeling very cranky. He knew all of Hannah Montana's songs by heart, and it wasn't because he was a faithful fan. "You'd feel the same way if you had to sit backstage listening to songs you've heard a thousand times," he complained. "I get it, you 'got nerve.'"

"Yes, I do," Miley agreed.

When the limo turned into their driveway, Miley was relieved. She couldn't wait to get away from her brother.

Jackson reached the front door first and started searching his pockets. "Hey, Mile, you got your key?" he asked.

Miley tossed her keys to Jackson. "Who's taking care of who?"

"Yeah, right," Jackson said as he walked into the house. "Sorry. Bye." He slammed the door.

"Jackson!" Miley shouted, banging on the door. "Come on, Jackson, let me in. Jackson!"

"Hey, Hannah!"

As Miley turned, a camera flash went off in her face. "Whoa!" she cried. The light was blinding. When she could see again, she recognized the photographer standing in front of her. His name was Paulie. And he was always after Hannah for a scoop.

"Gotcha!" he cried. "I knew if I followed you long enough, I'd find out where you live."

"Live? Here? Me?" Miley said, trying

to act innocent. "Oh! No! I-I-I . . . am just here to visit a friend," she finally stuttered.

Jackson opened the door. He was munching on a turkey leg.

"Looks more like a 'boyfriend' to me," Paulie said slyly.

With his mouth full of turkey, Jackson looked dumbfounded. "A-wha?" Then he realized what was happening. He pulled Miley into the house, holding up his arm to block their faces from the camera lens. But it didn't help.

"Say 'front page'!" Paulie exclaimed.

The camera flashed again, catching Jackson and Miley looking secretive and startled—like a romantic couple who had suddenly been found out. Paulie ran to his car, knowing that he had just taken a prize photo.

* * *

When Jackson walked into the living room the next morning, he could hear people outside. It's those photographers, he thought. He yelled toward the door, "Go away!" But when they heard his voice, the paparazzi began calling out to get his attention.

"Hey, boyfriend!"

"Smile, boyfriend!"

"Over here!"

Jackson was annoyed. He lifted the blind on the door and stared at the mob outside. "You guys wanna see something?" Jackson called back to them. "I'll show you a little something!" He made a silly face and did some monkey movements, then dropped the blind.

"Oh, great," Miley said as she walked into the living room. She had already seen the front-page story in a tabloid newspaper with a headline that read, HANNAH'S NEW MAN-NAH. "I can see the next headline, HANNAH DATES MONKEY BOY!"

"There wouldn't even be any headlines if it wasn't for you," Jackson said.

"And there wouldn't be any picture if you hadn't locked me out!" Miley shouted.

They both stopped arguing when they heard a commotion outside the house. Mr. Stewart was home, and the paparazzi were not making it easy for him to get to the front door.

"Clear it! Outta my way! This is my house, get back!" he yelled as he made his way to the house. When he got to the door, he turned back to face the crowd. "Hey, why don't you go chasing a crooked politician—at least he'd smile for you!"

When Mr. Stewart finally got inside, he saw Miley and Jackson. "So when exactly were you two going to tell me you were dating?" he asked with a chuckle.

"Dad, this isn't funny," Miley said. "It's horrible."

"Yeah, how could anyone believe I'd go out with anyone like her?" Jackson asked.

"Hey, it would be the luckiest day of your life if you got to date Hannah Montana," Miley countered. Then she realized what she had just said. "And what am I saying?"

Mr. Stewart held up the newspaper he was holding in his hand and admired the front-page photo of his children. "Well, the two of you do make a lovely couple," he said.

"Ewww!" Miley cried.

"Yechh!" Jackson exclaimed. He turned to Miley. "This is all your fault!" Then in his best Miley voice he said, "Don't bother with switching limos. No one's following us—I am so smart."

Mr. Stewart suddenly stopped smiling. "Is that true, Mile?"

"Dad, please, no lectures," Miley begged. "The entire world now thinks I'm dating Jackson. Isn't that punishment enough?"

"I'm afraid this time you're not going to be able to joke your way out of this one," her dad said. Then he went into the kitchen.

"Who's joking?" Miley said as he walked away. Just then, her cell phone rang. Looking down at the caller display, Miley moaned. "Oh, great, just what I need." She reluctantly flipped open the phone. "Hi, Traci."

Traci was Hannah Montana's friend—not Miley's. That meant she didn't know the truth about Hannah Montana's identity.

"Hannah, I can't believe you have a boyfriend and didn't tell me," Traci said. "And he's sooooo cute."

Looking over at Jackson, Miley watched her brother pick a large piece of lint out of his belly button. "Yeah, he's really . . . something," she said.

"You have to bring him to the party I'm throwing for Madonna tomorrow afternoon," Traci said. "Everyone's going to be there. It's the perfect place to show off Hannah's new hottie."

Miley panicked. "Traci, I don't know how . . ." Then she had an idea. She changed her attitude in mid-sentence. ". . . we could pass up an opportunity like this. Of course me and my—" Miley paused and then cringed as she said the next word. "—*hottie* will be at your party."

Jackson, who was still fascinated with

his belly-button lint, looked up. "What?!" he cried.

Miley put her hand over the phone to block Jackson's protest. Luckily, Traci didn't hear a thing.

"Fabu!" Traci said. "Ciao."

As Miley hung up the phone, Jackson moaned. "Will this nightmare never end?"

"Not until the press gets a picture of us breaking up," Miley told him. "And that party is the perfect place to do it."

"I am not going to some stupid celebrity party as Hannah's little show dog," Jackson said. He appealed to his dad. "Right, Dad?" But Mr. Stewart was giving him *The Look*. It was a look that meant *you need to do this*. "Dad?" Mr. Stewart kept staring at him—then he touched the rim of his cap, a sure sign that he was serious. "Oh, no, Dad! Why?"

Mr. Stewart walked over to Jackson. "Son, I know your sister got herself into this pickle, but she can't get out of it without your help," he explained. "You may not like it, but this is what family does for family."

Jackson knew that he had to give in. "All right, fine," he said. He gave Miley a hard stare. "But since you got me into this, I get to break up with you."

"No way," Miley argued. "I'm the teen pop sensation. I get to break up with you." Now it was Miley's turn to appeal to Mr. Stewart. "Right, Dad?" Oh, no, it was *The Look* again! "Dad?" Her dad couldn't be serious, could he? Then he touched his baseball cap! "Oh, no, Dad! Why?"

This photo nightmare was getting worse all the time! Not only did Hannah's fans think that Jackson was her boyfriend, but now he was going to break up with her!

Chapter Two

At Rico's snack bar, Lilly was sitting at a table, reading the newspaper. "Boy, life sure can be weird," she said. "Who'd have thought Miley'd be dating Jackson and . . ." Lilly looked over at Oliver. ". . . you'd be burping a sack of flour."

Oliver put a sack of flour on his shoulder as if he were burping a baby. His class had been told they needed to "adopt" a bag of flour and treat it as if it were a child in order to learn how difficult parenting was. He had done everything he could to make this experience as realistic as possible. The sack even wore a bonnet.

"Oliver," Lilly said, "the assignment is to raise a fake baby, you don't get extra credit for turning into Daddy McDork." She pointed to the utility belt he was wearing, which had powder and wipes tucked into the pockets.

"Hey, when you take Mr. Meyer's class next semester, you can handle the assignment any way you want," he told her. "But I'm going to take it seriously."

"Why?" Lilly asked.

"There's my little cuddle-wuddles!" Sarah called. Sarah, a girl in Oliver's class, walked over carrying a diaper bag. "Mommy got you some organic strained beets from a nonprofit Native American commune," she said to the bag of flour.

"Oooh, yummy," Oliver cooed. He looked over at Sarah. "You missed it, sweetheart," he said as he set the flour on the table. "He just learned how to sit up on his own."

"Good for you!" Sarah exclaimed, applauding the little sack of flour. "It won't be long before you're all grown up and making alternative fuel out of raisins!"

Suddenly Lilly understood why Oliver was so into this project. "Sooo, that's what this is all about," she said to him. As she watched how he acted around Sarah, it was obvious that he really liked the "mother" of his flour sack!

"What?" Oliver asked innocently.

"Nothing," Lilly answered. "It's just that you and Sarah and your *flour child* make a very cute family."

"Thank you," Sarah said, beaming. Then she dug around in her diaper bag for something.

"Oh, Lilly, you kidder," Oliver said, a little louder than necessary. "We're just friends doing an assignment. Nothing more." When he saw that Sarah wasn't paying attention, Oliver leaned over and whispered to Lilly. "Don't blow this for me. I really like her."

"Since when?" Lilly asked.

"Since she became the mother of my assignment," Oliver said with great sincerity.

Lilly gave her friend a "get real" look. Oliver shrugged in response.

"Look, I can't explain it," he said. "But the more time I spend with her, the more I like her."

He and Lilly looked over at Sarah who

was lovingly stroking the sack of flour.

"Oliver, I'm worried," Sarah said. "I think he looks a little pale."

Lilly had to laugh. "Of course he's pale," she blurted out. "He's bleached flour!"

Miley, dressed as Hannah, walked with Jackson into Traci's party. It was being held outdoors in a large tent that felt like a lavish ballroom. Jackson was wearing a hip jacket and an untucked shirt—a straight-from-the-runway look. They both smiled and nodded at the other guests as they made their entrance.

"Okay, so we're clear with the plan, right?" Miley whispered to Jackson. "We get in front of the press. I go, 'Jackson, what are you trying to say to me?' And you say—"

Jackson cut her off. "See ya, wouldn't

wanna be ya." Then he surveyed the room. "Where's the free shrimp?" A waiter walked by carrying a tray of drinks. Jackson grabbed a soda.

Miley was annoyed. "Jackson, you're breaking up with Hannah Montana," she said. "Can't you do this with a little more class?"

Her brother gave her a look and then belched in her face!

"Apparently not," Miley said with a sigh.

Just then, Traci came running up to them. She was all decked out in her party outfit, complete with a tiara. The cat she was holding wore a matching tiara.

"Look who came to wish you a happy birthday, Madonna," Traci squealed to the cat. "America's new sweethearts."

Jackson's eyes widened. "Madonna's a cat?" He looked around at the party scene. "I'm at a birthday party in a tent for a cat?"

His eyes rested on the gift table in the corner. A variety of cat items decorated with bows were spread out there. "What's for dessert, chocolate mousse or chocolate mouse?" he joked.

Traci, who was eager to like Hannah Montana's new boyfriend, smiled at Jackson. "You're funny," she said. Then she whispered to Miley. "And he's even cuter in person!"

"He is?" Miley said in disbelief. She was surprised Traci would say that, but then she caught herself. Jackson was supposed to be her new boyfriend. She smiled at Traci. "I mean he is, of course, he is. After all, he's my . . ." Miley stopped speaking. She mustered up her best acting skills and then finished her sentence. ". . . boyfriend."

By this point, Jackson was no longer paying attention to what the girls were saying. He was more interested in the shrimp. He was tossing them in the air and catching them in his mouth.

"Impressive," Traci cooed, watching Jackson eat. "Madonna's purring." Then she giggled. "Oh, wait, that's me!"

Jackson sniffed the air. "Oh, I smell something wrapped in bacon," he said. And he was off in search of more food.

"What a caveman!" Traci cried, swooning over Jackson. "You better be careful, someone's going to steal him."

"Make me an offer," Miley said.

Standing at the table, eating more shrimp and appetizers, Jackson didn't notice a guy walk up to him.

"So, you're Hannah's new dude," the guy said. "Awesome."

"Yeah, great," Jackson said through a mouthful of food. "Whatever."

"I'm Stavros," he said, extending his hand. "I'm dating Ashley."

Jackson looked around. "Which Ashley?"

Stavros laughed. "Like it matters," he said. "I've got courtside seats for the Lakers tomorrow night and Leonardo can't go. Wanna come?"

Cool! thought Jackson. Then he hesitated. "Do I have to pay for parking?"

"Hey, you're one of us now," Stavros replied. "We don't have to pay for any-thing."

"What do you mean?" Jackson asked.

Stavros leaned closer. "Dude," he con-fided, "when you're in the public eye as much as we are, companies give you stuff just for the publicity." He took off the sunglasses that were perched on the top of his head and handed them to Jackson. "Here. Get your picture taken wearing these and you'll be getting tons of glasses for free."

Jackson put on the cool sunglasses. "Awesome," he said.

Stavros pulled out an identical pair of glasses from his pocket and put them on. "Oh, yeah," he said.

Both of them stood looking around the room, bobbing their heads up and down.

Meanwhile, Traci and Miley were surveying the presents on the gift table.

"Look, Hannah," Traci said. "Someone got Madonna a rhinestone scooper!"

Miley was starting to get annoyed. She wanted to get on with the breakup. "Yeah," she said, "what a lucky kitty." She looked around the party. "Where's the press?"

Traci grinned at her. "Don't worry," she said. "I knew you'd want your privacy, so I kept the whole thing on the DL."

"Terrific," Miley managed to say. She forced a smile. Then she pointed to a lady in the corner. "Isn't that woman wearing the same dress as you?"

Gasping in horror, Traci shouted, "Oh, she has got to go! Security, escort my mother out!"

As Traci took off to take care of her fashion emergency, Miley ducked behind a plant and pulled out her cell phone. She had to take matters into her own hands. She did the best Traci imitation that she could and said, "Hello, *This Week in Hollywood*? It's Traci Van Horne and you'll never guess who's at my party. Hannah Montana and her new beau. . . . That's right. Oooh, and you better hurry. Ciao."

Now, this better work! Miley thought. She popped a shrimp in her mouth and waited for the press to arrive.

Chapter Three

Lilly couldn't believe how great the waves were that morning! With her board under her arm, she raced to find Oliver and tell him that the surf was definitely up. She found him at Rico's, buying bottles of water.

"Oliver, you've got to get your board," Lilly said as she ran up to him. "The waves are incredible today!"

Oliver wasn't listening. He was staring at Sarah, who was sitting at a table playing with their flour baby. She was making faces and kissing its little "belly." With a far-off look, he said wistfully, "How did I get so lucky?"

Lilly had an easy answer for that one. "Everyone picked partners, and you were the only two left," she told him.

"Ollie-kins!" Sarah called from her seat. "Where's the sunscreen? Now that they've destroyed the ozone layer, we have to protect little Ollie."

Oliver beamed with pride. "Coming, Sarah-boo!" he called back.

"Ollie-kins? Sarah-boo?" Lilly asked, rolling her eyes.

"I know," Oliver said. He got a little choked up. "My cup runneth over." He skipped over to Sarah and helped her put sunscreen all over the bag of flour.

Sarah proudly put her arm around Oliver.

"Just think, one day he could be a great humanitarian," she said, gazing at the flour sack.

Lilly couldn't help but offer her own prediction. "Or a couple dozen cupcakes," she muttered.

Just as Lilly was rolling her eyes about Oliver and Sarah, Miley was trying not to reveal her true feelings about her "boyfriend." This wasn't easy, because she was surrounded by a group of party guests who were all dying to get the inside scoop on her new guy.

Gina, a real gossip, started with the question they all wanted to ask. "So is he a good kisser?"

"Ewww-wee . . ." was the first thing out of Miley's mouth. Then she remembered that these girls didn't have a clue who

Hannah Montana really was—or that Jackson was her brother! So she quickly added, "We haven't done that yet. We're taking it slow. *Real* slow." Just to make this absolutely clear, she added, "I'm talking centuries."

At that moment, Traci came running up, clutching Madonna in her arms and looking panicked.

"Hannah, train wreck!" she exclaimed, pulling Miley away from the group. "Someone tipped off the press that you were here."

Miley tried her best to act shocked. "No!" she cried. Then she glanced at the tent entrance and saw a group of paparazzi, including Paulie, trying to get into the party.

"I'm so embarrassed," Traci said. She grabbed Miley's hand. "I'll sneak you out the back."

"No, that would ruin everything!" Miley blurted out. Then she quickly covered by adding, "I mean, if we don't face them now, they'll never go away."

Once again, Traci was reminded of why she admired her friend Hannah Montana. "You are so brave."

The roar of a sports car and the squeal of tires filled the air. Miley could hear Jackson's voice.

"Whoa!" he hollered.

Stavros and Jackson walked into the party. Miley rushed over to her brother and pulled him aside. "Jackson, where've you been?"

"Stavros just let me drive his Vavetti convertible," he told her, pointing to his new friend. "It was awesome!"

"Why don't you keep it for the week?" Stavros said. "I've got an SUV that needs a little TLC." He tossed Jackson the keys to the Vavetti.

"Oh, yeah!" Jackson exclaimed, shaking Stavros's hand as if they were the best of buddies.

Miley couldn't believe what she was seeing. "Honey," she said through gritted teeth as she grabbed Jackson's arm.

Jackson gave Stavros a knowing look. "Chicks," he said. Stavros gave him an understanding nod in return.

When they finally had a moment alone, Jackson glared at Miley. "What?"

Miley led him to an area packed with press. As they approached the mob of microphones and cameras, Miley whispered to Jackson. "The press is here." Then she added, a little louder for the press to hear, "So if there's anything you would like to tell me, you should tell me now." She stood back and gave Jackson "center stage" for his breakup speech.

"Oh, right," Jackson said. Then he looked at the car keys in his hand and flipped them around.

Miley was getting impatient. "Come on, Jackson, what do you have to say to me?" she said, encouraging him.

"I, I . . ." Jackson stuttered.

Boy, Miley thought. He is really milking this moment! "Go ahead," she said. "I can handle it."

Paulie called out from the crowd. "Well, say something, monkey boy!"

A dozen flashbulbs went off as the photographers tried to get the perfect photo of Hannah Montana and her boyfriend.

Jackson took in the moment. He looked at the photographers. He looked at his sister. And then with heartfelt emotion he said, "I love you, Hannah Montana, and I never want to break up with you. Ever, ever!" Then he gave his sister a huge hug, as the photographers began snapping pictures and firing questions at them.

Miley was stuck. All she could say was, "Well, aren't you full of surprises . . . honey!"

The next morning, a choice photo of the new hot couple graced the papers again. This time the headline read, JACKSANNAH 4-EVER!

Jackson's public declaration of love had only made the press more interested in this new relationship—and made Miley even more miserable!

Chapter Four

That afternoon, Mr. Stewart was hanging out in the living room. He was relaxing, playing a few tunes on the piano . . . until Miley and Jackson came home. As they walked in the door, it was clear they were in the middle of a huge argument.

"Come on, Mile, what's the big deal?" Jackson was saying.

"Don't even talk to me!" Miley barked, putting up her hand. She was still dressed as Hannah Montana. She flipped her long hair at him.

Mr. Stewart looked up from the keyboard. "Sounds like you two are still a couple," he said with a chuckle.

"Oh, not just any couple!" Miley shouted. "According to Jackson, we're the happiest couple in Hollywood!"

Her father sighed. Clearly the big breakup that had been planned for Traci's party hadn't happened. "I'm going to ask a question I thought I'd never ask one of my kids," he said. "Jackson, why didn't you break up with your sister?"

Jackson told the truth right away. "All right, look, I admit it," he told his dad. "I may have gotten a little carried away. But, Dad, some guy loaned me his convertible for the week just because I'm Hannah's boyfriend."

"I don't care what the reason was," Mr. Stewart scolded. "You were supposed to help your sister and—"

"It's the Vavetti twin turbo," Jackson interrupted. He held up the car keys.

Mr. Stewart's face softened, and so did his voice. He switched gears as fast as that sports car. "—you and I are gonna take a long ride and talk about it. I'll drive." He took the keys from Jackson's hand and headed for the door. Jackson was right behind him.

"Hey, what about me?" Miley called.

"Come on, Mile, there's no backseat and you already had a ride," Mr. Stewart answered on his way to the front door.

"Do you hear yourself?" Miley asked her dad. He was as bad as Jackson!

"Sorry. Your daddy just had a male moment there," he apologized. He turned to his son. "Jackson, your sister's right. You can't take advantage of her like this."

Jackson was stunned. "Hey, she's the one who made me her boyfriend in the first place," he argued. "All I'm asking is that we keep pretending for one week so I can have a little fun with it." He looked right at his sister. "And you can't even give me that."

"Good!" Miley shouted. "We understand each other."

"Sure, we do," Jackson said. "When you need a favor from me, that's family helping family. But when I ask for a little something in return, suddenly Hannah doesn't play that game. Nice to know how things work around here."

With that, Jackson stomped up the stairs.

Miley was expecting to go a few more rounds with her brother. But his words were sinking in, and she started to feel bad.

"Don't worry, Mile," Mr. Stewart said, giving her a hug. "He'll cool off."

Miley sat down on the couch and looked up at her dad. "I know . . . it's just . . ."

Mr. Stewart sat down next to her. "What?" he asked.

"Well, I did get him into this, and he did help me out," Miley confessed. "And he never gets the perks I get when I'm Hannah. I mean, really, where's the harm?"

Her dad gave her a hard look. He was proud of her, but he wasn't too confident about this plan. "I don't know," he said. "But I'm sure the two of you will find it."

"I can't believe I'm going to say this," Miley said. "But I think I have to do it." She was resolved to stick with this new plan of pretending to be Jackson's girlfriend—

for a limited time. "One week. I can handle that."

"Yes!" Jackson screamed as he ran back into the living room. He gave Miley a huge hug. "You're the best girlfriend I've ever had!"

Mr. Stewart rubbed his head. "This is weirder than a three-eyed billy goat in a flatbed truck in the middle of Manhattan!"

Miley shrugged at her dad's comment but had to admit that the next week was going to be very, very strange!

Just as Miley had imagined, the week was a blur of the bizarre. She found herself being hugged by Jackson at tons of photo shoots. They went to club openings, movie premieres, and a yacht party. They walked the red carpet, rode in private jets, and got tons of free stuff. With each event, Jackson got more into his role, putting on only the hippest clothes and trendiest accessories. Miley was growing tired of the scene very quickly. To make matters worse, Jackson seemed to enjoy hanging out with Stavros. He was even worse than Jackson! And the two of them together were trouble. In the back of the limo, Miley sat between them as they both stared at their belly buttons!

Miley shook her head. How did she let herself get sucked into this mess? And even more important, how was she going to get her life back?

Chapter Five

Near the end of the week, Mr. Stewart was waiting for his kids to come home from another event, lunch at the opening of a new restaurant. He was on the phone with Jackson's best friend, Cooper, when he heard the Vavetti pull into the driveway.

"Okay, Coop, I'll tell him," Mr. Stewart said into the phone.

Miley, still dressed as Hannah, walked into the house. She looked exhausted.

"So, how was lunch with the boyfriend?" Mr. Stewart asked with a smirk.

"We didn't eat," Miley said and threw herself on the couch.

"Why not?" he asked.

Just then, Jackson walked through the front door. He was talking on his cell phone and dressed as if he had just walked off the pages of the trendiest Hollywood gossip magazine.

"No, no, no. You listen to me, Mr. Diddy," Jackson said angrily. "If you want us to eat at your restaurant again, it's table one or nothing." He was pacing around the room. "I don't care if you have to dump Brangelina. You're dealing with Jacksannah now. Good day . . . I said good day, Diddy!" And he hung up.

Miley looked over at her dad. "Answer your question?" she asked. Obviously, she had not gone to lunch with Jackson but with a celebrity monster!

Mr. Stewart had had about enough of this charade. "Hey, Jacksannah, Cooper called," he said. Just to make his point, he added, "You remember him, your best friend?"

"Oh, right," Jackson replied. "I've been meaning to get back to him." He pulled out his new cell phone and recorded a memo for himself. "Note to self," he said into the phone. "Send Coop a nice fruit basket saying I'm sorry, blah, blah, blah, and throw in an autographed photo of Jacksannah."

Now Miley had heard enough. "That's it! I've had it!" she yelled. "Look at yourself! I don't even know who you are anymore." Suddenly, Miley knew just what to do. "And tomorrow on the *Wake Up, It's Wendy!* show I'm announcing that 'Jacksannah' is history."

"Hold on, you can't do that," Jackson argued. "We had a deal. And if I'm not seen in public wearing the sunglasses, the jacket, and the watch, I'm going to have to give them all back!"

"I don't care!" Miley yelled.

"But the public doesn't want me, they want us," Jackson said, trying to appeal to her softer side. "I'm nothing without you. You complete me." He drew a little heart with his finger over his chest.

"And you completely creep me out!" Miley said.

"But what about family helping family?" Jackson asked, pleading.

"I tried to help you, but all it's done is turn you into an obnoxious, self-centered jerk who took advantage of his sister and blew off his best friend," Miley said as she walked toward the stairs. She stopped halfway and did her best Jackson super-star imitation. "Dude, it's over! Snoop Dorky Dork." Then she ran to her room.

"Hey, hey, I did not blow him off! I'm sending him a nice fruit basket!" Jackson called after her. "Dad, talk to her!" But when Jackson turned around, he saw that his dad was gone. "Dad?"

The roar of the Vavetti from the drive-way sent Jackson out the front door. As he opened the door, he heard his father yell from the car, "Yeeeeeeeeeee-ha!"

Jackson took out his fancy cell phone. "I am going to send you a very strongly worded text message," he said, punching the buttons.

Then he had to prepare for the TV show the next day. He couldn't let Hannah Montana break up with him—not just yet.

✳ ✳ ✳

At Rico's, another couple was having trouble with their relationship. Oliver and Sarah were sitting at a table, and the air was thick with tension. Sarah was busy knitting, and Oliver was pretending to read a magazine.

Finally, Sarah couldn't take the awkward silence. "So, how about that A we got on the baby project?" she asked.

"Yeah," Oliver said without excitement. "Pretty great . . ."

Sarah went back to her knitting, and Oliver looked down at his magazine. He turned a page and cleared his throat.

"You say something?" Sarah asked.

"No," Oliver said.

"Oh." Sarah sighed.

Oliver couldn't take the silence anymore. "I'm just going to go stretch my legs," he said, standing up.

"All right," Sarah said, not even looking up from her knitting.

Oliver walked over to the counter where Lilly was sitting. He leaned in to his friend and pointed to Sarah. "She's suffocating me!"

Lilly smirked. "Sarah?" she asked. "The love of your life? The apple of your eye? The mother of your flour?"

"That's just it," Oliver explained. "Without the kid we've got nothing to talk about."

"So tell her how you feel and get it over with," Lilly advised.

Oliver sighed. "Lilly, you don't understand," he said. "That would break her heart. I'm her Big Daddy Oken!"

Just as Oliver was explaining himself, Sarah tapped him on the shoulder.

"Big Daddy," Sarah said solemnly, "I've got to be honest. Without the baby we have nothing to talk about, you're boring, and you use petroleum-based hair products. It's over." Then she faced Lilly and gave her a big, bright smile. "Bye, Lilly!"

Lilly raised her eyebrows at Oliver.

"She's dying inside," he said.

Lilly rolled her eyes. Relationships were too hard to figure out!

Chapter Six

On the set of the *Wake Up, It's Wendy!*
show the next day, Hannah Montana was
singing her song, "If We Were a Movie."
Wendy was bopping to the catchy tune.
She had a huge grin pasted on her face and
looked as if she had downed a dozen extra-
large coffees.

At the end of the song, Miley took a
bow and the studio audience applauded
loudly. Wendy raced over to give her
morning guest a huge hug.

"What a beautiful, beautiful song! Sung by a beautiful, beautiful girl!" Wendy chirped. She faced the audience with hyper energy and grabbed a CD from a nearby table. "Take a look under your seats, people!" she hollered. "We all got free Hannah Montana goodie bags! Whoo!"

As the audience went wild for the freebies, Wendy led Miley over to the couch on the set for their interview.

"So, Hannah," Wendy said, trying to get personal with her star. "When I hear a song sung with that kind of emotion, I can't help thinking you were thinking about someone very special! Am I right, am I right?" She looked at her audience knowingly. "I'm right, aren't I?"

Miley was thankful that Wendy addressed the boyfriend subject right away. She wanted to get this all settled—and quickly. "Well, now that you bring it up," she confided to the talk show host. "I do have some news about me and . . . Jackson."

Wendy beamed at the thought that Hannah Montana was about to make a major romantic announcement on her show! The audience hooted and howled their excitement.

"No, no, no, it's not like that," Miley said quickly. "It's really kind of serious."

The audience quickly changed its collective chorus to questioning *Oooh's*.

Miley took a deep breath. "The truth is," she said, "Jackson and I are—"

Before Miley could finish her sentence, Jackson appeared on the set. He was decked out in a new racing jacket. He had sunglasses perched on the top of his head and wore an expensive Grunschwiegenflagen watch. He finished Miley's sentence for her. "—totally and completely in love!"

The audience screamed wildly.

Miley whipped her head around to glare at Jackson. "Oh, no," she said. He was going to ruin this plan, too? Then Jackson jumped on the couch, raising his hands like a boxer and bouncing up and down.

With crazed enthusiasm, he yelled, "I love Hannah Montana! I love Hannah Montana! I LOVE HANNAH MONTANA!" He unzipped his jacket to show that he was wearing a Jacksannah T-shirt. It was a photo of Jackson and Hannah's faces in a heart.

The crowd squealed with delight.

Wendy was ecstatic! She loved having the scoop on hot entertainment news. She turned to the audience. "Ladies and gentlemen, the couple of the moment, Jacksannah! Whoo!"

The audience screamed even louder.

Miley pulled Jackson down onto the couch. "What are you doing?" she whispered.

"I'm trying to save this relationship!" Jackson said, speaking to the audience.

"What relationship?" Miley demanded, gritting her teeth.

Jackson stretched out his arms to the audience. "I love this woman! Even more than I love my—" He held up his wrist. "—Grunschwiegenflagen watch! Water resistant to a hundred and fifty meters."

On the set, only Wendy seemed to be impressed. "Wow, Hannah," she said. "What do you have to say to that?"

"You want to know what I'm going to say?" Miley said. She was at her boiling point and ready to scream!

Wendy and the audience started to chant, "Yes! Yes! Yes!"

Jackson pointed to his jacket and watch, then he mimed driving the Vavetti, just in case Miley had forgotten that she had told him he could enjoy the celebrity good life for a little while longer.

"You make me sick," Miley said.

The audience gasped in shock. Wendy fell back on the couch.

Miley forgot all about the audience. This was between her and her brother. "I hate everything you've become," she shouted. "I never should've started this dating thing. It was one big, huge mistake, but now it's over!"

But Jackson was not ready for this gig to end. "No, no, I can change!" he begged, on his knees. "Please, give me another chance! I don't want to lose you—and all the things." Then he looked right at the camera. "Grunschwiegenflagen watch," he said, making sure that the watch got its product placement on the show. "We have so much together!" he said to Miley.

She started to walk off the set. "Forget it! We have nothing together," she replied. "Jackson, it's over!"

A collective "Noooooo!" came from the audience.

Wendy tried to play relationship counselor. "Hannah, he's on his knees! How can you turn him down?"

"Watch me!" Miley shouted as she started to head backstage.

Jackson followed Miley on his knees, singing the lyrics to the song she had sung earlier on the show.

Miley turned and saw the celebrity creep that her brother had turned into. "Look at yourself!" she yelled. "You're pathetic!"

Suddenly, Miley realized that she wasn't

just Miley Stewart at home, fighting with her annoying older brother. She was appearing on a TV show as Hannah Montana. The sudden silence on the set made her painfully aware how harsh those words sounded coming from Jackson's "girlfriend."

The audience's silence changed to booing and cries of, "You're cruel!" And worst yet, the Hannah Montana goodie bags were being flung on the stage in an angry flurry.

"Wait! Stop!" Miley called to the audience as she dodged the bags. "Please! You don't understand!"

Immediately the crowd started chanting, "Jackson, Jackson!"

Miley was stunned and hurt to see how the audience had turned on her. But there was nothing she could do now. She looked over at Jackson. "Thanks a lot," she said as she headed offstage, away from the crowd.

Jackson took in the audience's reaction. Then he looked at Miley, walking slowly offstage. He waved his hand to quiet the crowd. "Hold on, everybody," he said. "I got something I gotta say. Hannah's not the bad guy here. I am. I wanted a taste of the good life, and she pretended to go out with me so I could get it. The truth is, there never really was a Jacksannah."

There were lots of whispers in the audience. Now everyone was confused.

Wendy stepped in and asked Jackson a direct question to clear things up. "So you're saying all of this was pretend?"

"Well, not all of it," he confessed. "I do love Hannah," he said. "But like a sister. And I was hoping we can get back to that." He looked over at Miley hopefully. "I really am sorry."

Miley smiled. "Okay," she said.

"*Awwwwww,*" the audience cried together.

Wendy started a chant. "Hug, hug, hug, hug . . ." The audience joined in, and Miley and Jackson happily hugged.

After a moment, Jackson pulled out of the hug so that his watch was in line with the camera. Again, he pointed to it as if he were an old pro at TV endorsements.

"Stop pointing at the watch!" Miley scolded.

"Sorry," Jackson said. He just couldn't help one more acknowledgment of his celebrity bling. It was his last moment of living the good life!

Jackson's dreams of being in the spotlight with all the cool free stuff were over, and so were Oliver's aspirations to being a parent with Sarah. Oliver was sitting at the counter at Rico's, feeling down. Then he spotted a dad walking by with a baby in an infant carrier. Oliver got a wistful look on his face. He remembered all the fun times he'd had with his flour baby. The little guy had looked so sweet with his hat on, so adorable when he was swinging in his swing, so lovable when Oliver would hold him up and spin him around. The flour child also played baseball with him. Oliver had set him up with a mitt and everything. Best of all, though, Oliver had loved just hanging out with the flour baby on the beach—just the two of them.

Well, Oliver thought, at least he'd had a taste of the good life.

Don't miss the next awesome Hannah Montana book!

Sweet Revenge

Based on the series created by Michael Poryes and Rich Correll & Barry O'Brien

Part One is based on the episode, "The Idol Side of Me," Written by Douglas Lieblein

Part Two is based on the episode, "Schooly Bully," Written by Douglas Lieblein & Heather Wordham

When mean girls Amber and Ashley put out their annual Cool List, Miley and Lilly are at the bottom. So Miley plans to humiliate Amber on national TV and soon learns that revenge isn't really all that sweet!

Plus, when a new girl turns out to be the scariest school bully ever, Miley enlists her bodyguard Roxy to keep her safe. But soon she has to decide which is worse: being bullied . . . or being bossed around!